WALTUR PAINTS HIMSELF INTO A CORNER
AND OTHER STORIES

by Barbara Gregorich
Illustrated by Kristin Sorra

Houghton Mifflin Company
Boston 2007

www.houghtonmifflinbooks.com

The text of this book is set in Leawood Book.
The illustrations are in pen and ink and watercolor.

Library of Congress Cataloging-in-Publication Data

Gregorich, Barbara.
Waltur paints himself into a corner and other stories / written by Barbara Gregorich and illustrated by Kristin Sorra.
p. cm.
Summary: Walter the bear learns more lessons from his friend Matilda, such as "do not put the cart before the horse" and "let sleeping dogs lie."
ISBN-13: 978-0-618-74796-2 (hardcover)
ISBN-10: 0-618-74796-6 (hardcover)
[1. Bears—Fiction. 2. Animals—Fiction. 3. Proverbs—Fiction.] I. Sorra, Kristin, ill.
II. Title.
PZ7.G8613Wai 2007
[Fic]—dc22
2006102370

Printed in Singapore
TWP 10 9 8 7 6 5 4 3 2 1

CONTENTS

WALTUR

PUTS THE CART BEFORE THE HORSE

Matilda baked a blueberry pie
for the Summer Fair.
Waltur baked a honey cake.
"I must write a thank-you speech," he said.

“Thank you for what?” asked Matilda.

“Thank you for the ribbon,” explained Waltur.

“Ribbon?” asked Matilda. “What ribbon?”

“The ribbon for First Prize in Sweets,” said Waltur.

Matilda sighed.

“First,” she said, “you must win.
Then, if you win, you can give a speech.”

Matilda left to carry her blueberry pie to the fair.
Waltur wrote a long speech.
Then he hurried out the door,
carrying his cake and speech.

He met a horse and cart on the road.
"I must hurry to the Summer Fair," Waltur told the horse. "Can you give me a ride?"
"Hop in," said the horse.

Waltur sat in the cart and the horse pulled.
"Faster," said Waltur.
"No problem," said the horse.
The horse trotted up a steep hill.
The horse slowed down.
"Pull," said Waltur. "Pull faster."

The horse looked around at Waltur.
"You are a bear," said the horse.
"You are heavy."
"Pull," Waltur said again. "Pull faster."
The horse stopped.
"You're so smart," said the horse,
"*you* pull the cart!"

"I have a better idea," said Waltur.
He unhitched the cart and moved it
to the front of the horse.
"Push," he said. "Push fast."

"Not a good idea," said the horse
as it pushed the cart uphill.
"Yes," argued Waltur. "The cart will get to
the fair sooner because it is in front."
"All wrong," grumbled the horse. "All wrong."
The hill grew steeper and steeper.
"I can't see a thing," said the horse.
"We are almost there!" shouted Waltur.

The horse gave a mighty push.
And then — the cart began
to roll down the hill.
Faster . . . and faster
. . . and faster!
The horse watched.

Waltur's honey cake flew out of the cart.

His speech flew into the air.

"E-yow!" shouted Waltur. *"E-yoooowwwwww!"*

Everyone at the Summer Fair looked up.

Sheets of paper floated
down from the sky.
"It's a snowstorm!"
shouted the squirrels.

The cart flipped end over end.
"It's a Ferris wheel!"
shouted the rabbits.

Waltur sailed through the air.
"It's a flying carpet!"
shouted the badgers.

FAIR
the best cake
in the world

Waltur climbed down
from the tree in which
he had landed.

"My honey cake smashed to pieces,"
he told Matilda.
"Now I won't win First Prize for Sweets.
I should have put first things first."
Matilda brought Waltur a cold lemonade.
"You put the cart before the horse," she said.
The judges awarded Matilda's blueberry pie
First Prize in Sweets.
"Thank you," said Matilda.

The judges circled Waltur.
"Great colors!" they told him.
"Great sounds, great action! What a show!
"We award you Grand Prize
for Best of the Summer Fair."
"Me?" asked Waltur. "I win the Grand Prize?"
"Yes," said all the judges.
"But I don't have a speech to give," said Waltur.
"You are such a modest bear," said the judges.

WALTUR

PAINTS HIMSELF INTO A CORNER

Waltur carried
a chair outdoors.
He carried another
chair outdoors.
He carried a table
and a lamp outdoors.
"What are you doing?"
asked Matilda.
"I am going to paint
the floor," said Waltur.

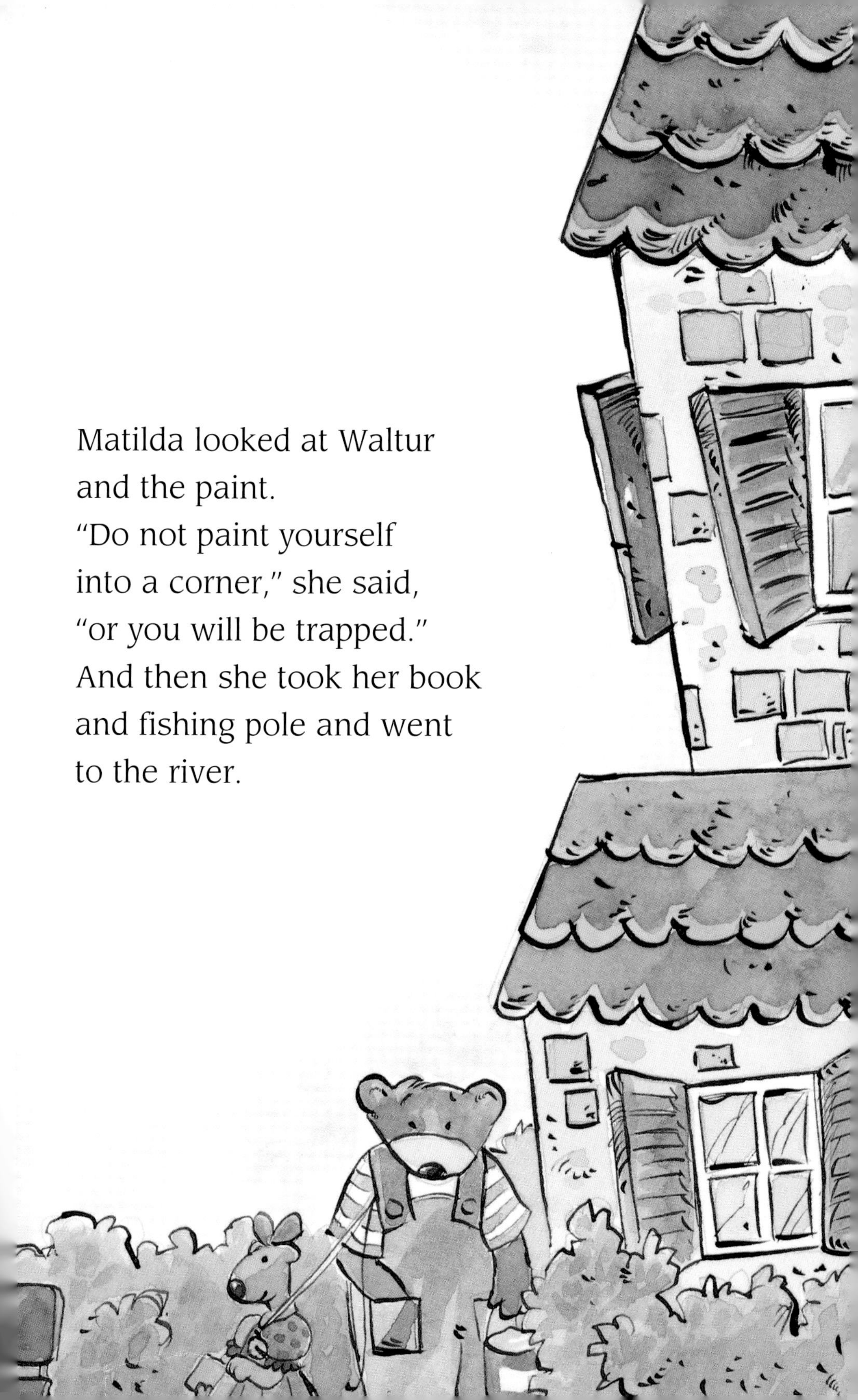

Matilda looked at Waltur
and the paint.
“Do not paint yourself
into a corner,” she said,
“or you will be trapped.”
And then she took her book
and fishing pole and went
to the river.

Waltur marched up to the first corner
and painted it.
At first he painted the corner small.
I have painted the corner
and I am not trapped, he thought.
So he painted the corner larger.
Darwin came to visit.
"I am painting the floor," Waltur told him.

“I must think as I work,” said Waltur.
“I must not let the corners trap me.”
“I will sit outside,” said Darwin.

A goat came to visit.
So did a fox, and so did a badger.
Darwin's pig came by.
"Waltur does not want the corners to trap him,"
Darwin explained.
They all sat outside and watched Waltur work.
"Go, Waltur!" shouted Darwin.

Waltur finished the second and third corners.
"Painting is hard work," he said.
"Keep going," cheered the goat. "You can do it."
"Anything can happen," warned the fox.

Waltur dipped his brush
into the paint.
"I have painted three
corners already,"
he told the crowd.
"And I did not paint
myself into them."
"Hot dog!"
shouted the pig.
"Go, Waltur!"
cheered Darwin.
At last Waltur painted
the fourth corner.

"There!" said Waltur. "All four corners are painted.
Now I will come out and play."
Suddenly everyone was silent.
"Uh-oh," said the goat.
"Uh-oh," said Darwin, the pig, the badger, and the fox.

Waltur looked down.
He was standing in an unpainted circle.
All around him, the floor was covered
in wet paint.
He had painted himself into the center
of the room.
"Help!" shouted Waltur. "I am trapped!"

"You will have to wait for the paint to dry,"
said the badger.
"But that is not interesting to watch,"
said the fox.
"So we will go play," said the goat.
Waltur sat alone in the center of the room.

Matilda came home with a whole string of fish.
"Uh-oh," she said.
"I did not paint myself into a corner," said Waltur.
"But I did paint myself into a place
I can't get out of."
Matilda held the fishing pole across the floor.
"Have some fish," she said.
"Thank you," said Waltur.
And then Matilda read to Waltur
until the paint dried.

WALTUR

WON'T LET SLEEPING DOGS LIE

"What a beautiful day!" shouted Waltur.
"Let's go for a walk!"
"I haven't had breakfast yet," said Matilda.
"Breakfast can wait," said Waltur. "Let's walk."
Waltur led the way to Darwin's house.

"Wake up, Darwin!" he shouted.
Darwin woke up and came along.
The three friends walked by the farmer's fields.
"Wake up, bull!" shouted Waltur.
The bull turned and looked at Waltur.
Waltur saw the farmer's dog
sleeping on the porch.
"Wake up, dog!" he shouted. "Enjoy the day!"

"It's better to let sleeping dogs lie," said Matilda.
"Why?" asked Waltur.
"The dog might wake up in a bad mood,"
she said. "Sometimes it is best
to leave things as they are."
So the friends filed past the sleeping dog
and had a wonderful walk.

The next morning
was also beautiful.
"What a day!"
shouted Waltur.
"Let's go for a walk!"
"I am going to eat
my breakfast,"
said Matilda.
Waltur pounded
on Darwin's door.
"Let's go for a walk!"
he shouted.
Darwin pulled down
the blinds and went
back to sleep.

Waltur walked by the farmer's fields.
"Wake up, bull!" he shouted.
The bull snorted and shook its horns at Waltur.
Waltur saw the farmer's dog
sleeping on the porch.
It would be fun to walk with a dog by my side,
he thought.
"Wake up, dog!" shouted Waltur.
"What a day!"
The dog kept on sleeping.

Waltur stepped onto the porch.
"Wake up, dog," he said.
The dog kept on sleeping.

Waltur poked the dog.
"Wake up," he said.
"Snarl!"
The dog jumped to its feet.
"Grrrrrrrr!" it growled.
And then it jumped at Waltur.

Waltur jumped off the porch
and ran down the path.
"Grrrr! Grrrr! Grrrr!"
The dog snapped at Waltur's heels.
"Yip! Yip! Yip!"
The dog's puppies chased Waltur, too.

The farmer ran out of his house.
"Get that bear!" he shouted.
The farmer's helper heard the noise.
He chased Waltur with a tractor.

Waltur raced down the road.
The bull got loose and joined the chase.
"Help!" shouted Waltur as he ran.

"Grrrr! Grrrr! Grrrr!"
The dog was about to bite Waltur—
but Waltur jumped into the river!
He swam to the other side, crawled out,
and ran into the forest.

At last he stopped.
Waltur was wet.
And — he was lost!
Day turned into night.
Waltur sat with his head
in his hands.
"What a day," he sighed.
"What a day."
Then he saw a light.

The light came closer.
It was Matilda, with a flashlight and food.
"There you are," she said.
"I'll bet you are hungry."
"I woke up a sleeping dog," Waltur admitted
as he ate sandwiches and blueberry pie.
"I got chased," he said. "I got wet.
And I got lost. From now on,
I will let sleeping dogs lie."

Waltur and Matilda walked home
through the dark forest.
They were careful not to wake anybody.

FUNNY ENGLISH SAYINGS

The sayings in this book are idioms. Such sayings have been around for hundreds of years because they express truths about life.

Don't put the cart before the horse —
This five-hundred-year-old saying warns us not to do things in the wrong order.

Don't paint yourself into a corner —
Nobody is quite sure where this saying came from, but there are many sayings about corners. If you are forced into a corner, somebody else traps you. But when you paint yourself into a corner, you trap yourself.

Let sleeping dogs lie — This seven-hundred-year-old saying may have come about when somebody accidentally awakened a watchdog. The advice here is, don't make trouble if you don't have to.

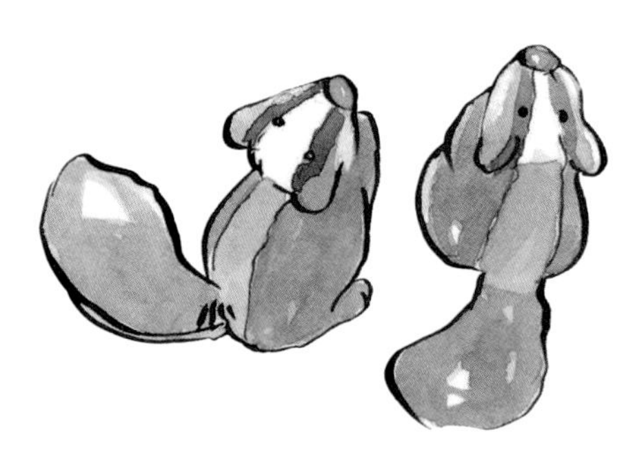